To: Mirabelle – Enjoy

From: Donna + Murray Hostetter

Enjoy the Baby Dill Story!

Best wishes,
Bob Salton

DEDICATION

This book is dedicated to my grandchildren, William, Alexandra, Peter and Leta.
Pickle Bumps for Baby Dill was a response to their request to "tell us a story about a pickle."
It rapidly became one of their favorites and their enthusiasm provided the inspiration that led to its publication.

~Robert Fulton

ACKNOWLEDGEMENTS

I am deeply indebted to my wife, Jackie, without whose support and encouragement this work could not have been completed. I would also like to thank John Martin of Bellwether Media for his insights and suggestions during the development of this book and the many friends and family members who offered their ideas and support.

Special thanks are due to Seal and Corinne Dwyer of North Star Press for their help and guidance in preparing this book for publication.

~Robert Fulton

www.picklebumppress.com

ISBN: 978-0-9845559-0-1

Published by Pickle Bump Press, Avon, Minnesota

Printed in the United States of America by Sentinel Printing Company, Inc., St. Cloud, Minnesota

First Printing: May 2010

All materials are warranted to be free from hazardous materials under the
United States Consumer Product Safety Improvement Act (CPSIA).

PICKLE BUMPS FOR BABY DILL

Story by Bob Fulton
Illustrations by Melissa Meyer

PICKLE BUMP PRESS
Avon, Minnesota

Jill Dill and Bill Dill lived in a little town called Pickleville. They were expecting a baby and they were very excited.

WELCOME TO
PiCKLEViLLE
POP: 876

Jill Dill had a great big tummy and inside her tummy Baby Dill was growing.
Bill said, "Hey Jill, do you know what? Before long you are going to be a Mama."
Jill answered, "I know, and pretty soon you will be a Papa!"

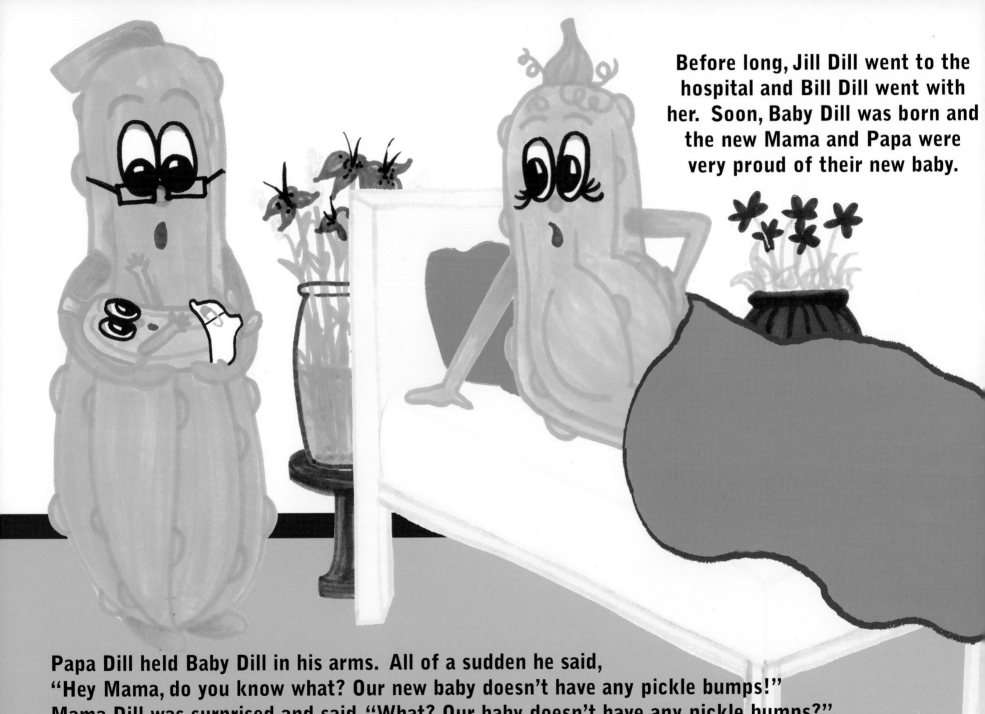

Before long, Jill Dill went to the hospital and Bill Dill went with her. Soon, Baby Dill was born and the new Mama and Papa were very proud of their new baby.

Papa Dill held Baby Dill in his arms. All of a sudden he said,
"Hey Mama, do you know what? Our new baby doesn't have any pickle bumps!"
Mama Dill was surprised and said, "What? Our baby doesn't have any pickle bumps?"
Papa Dill answered, "No. Not even one!"
Mama Dill said, "Maybe the pickle bumps will grow when Baby Dill gets older."

As Baby Dill grew older, Mama Dill and Papa Dill noticed that Baby Dill still did not have any pickle bumps. Mama Dill asked, "Do you think Baby Dill will ever get any pickle bumps?" Papa Dill said, "I don't really know."

Before long Baby Dill had grown to be big enough to go outside to play with the neighborhood friends.

One day, while standing on the sidelines of the soccer field, one of the friends said, "Hey Baby Dill, you look different than the other dill pickle friends. You don't have any pickle bumps."

Baby Dill said tearfully, "Yes, I know."

The friend took Baby Dill's hand and said, "That's okay, you don't really need pickle bumps."

Baby Dill said, "Thanks, but I still really, really want some."

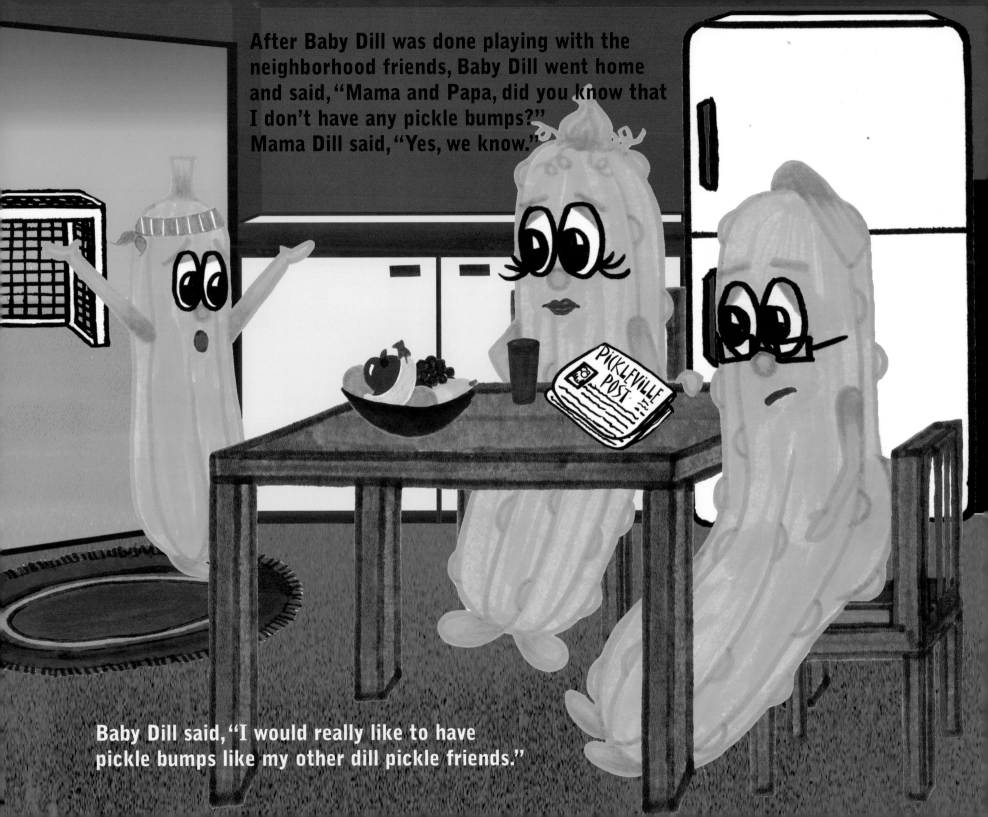

After Baby Dill was done playing with the neighborhood friends, Baby Dill went home and said, "Mama and Papa, did you know that I don't have any pickle bumps?"
Mama Dill said, "Yes, we know."

Baby Dill said, "I would really like to have pickle bumps like my other dill pickle friends."

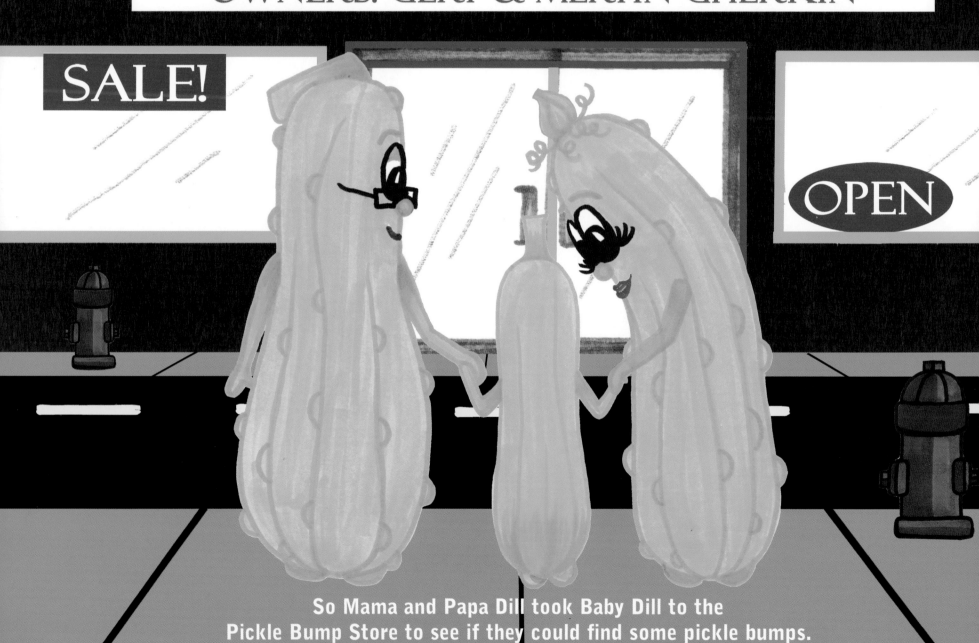

So Mama and Papa Dill took Baby Dill to the
Pickle Bump Store to see if they could find some pickle bumps.

Gert and Mertin Gherkin's Pickle Bump Store had lots of pickle bumps.
Mama Dill said, "We need some pickle bumps for Baby Dill.
Do you have any that are the right size and the right color?"

They found some that were just the right size and color for Baby Dill. Mama and Papa Dill bought the pickle bumps, and then Mama Dill asked, "How do we put on the pickle bumps?" Gert Gherkin said, "You will need some pickle bump glue, but we don't have any. Brad and Betty Sweetpickle own a Pickle Bump Glue Store and may have pickle bump glue for you."

So Mama and Papa Dill took Baby Dill to see if Brad and Betty Sweetpickle's Pickle Bump Glue Store had the right pickle bump glue.

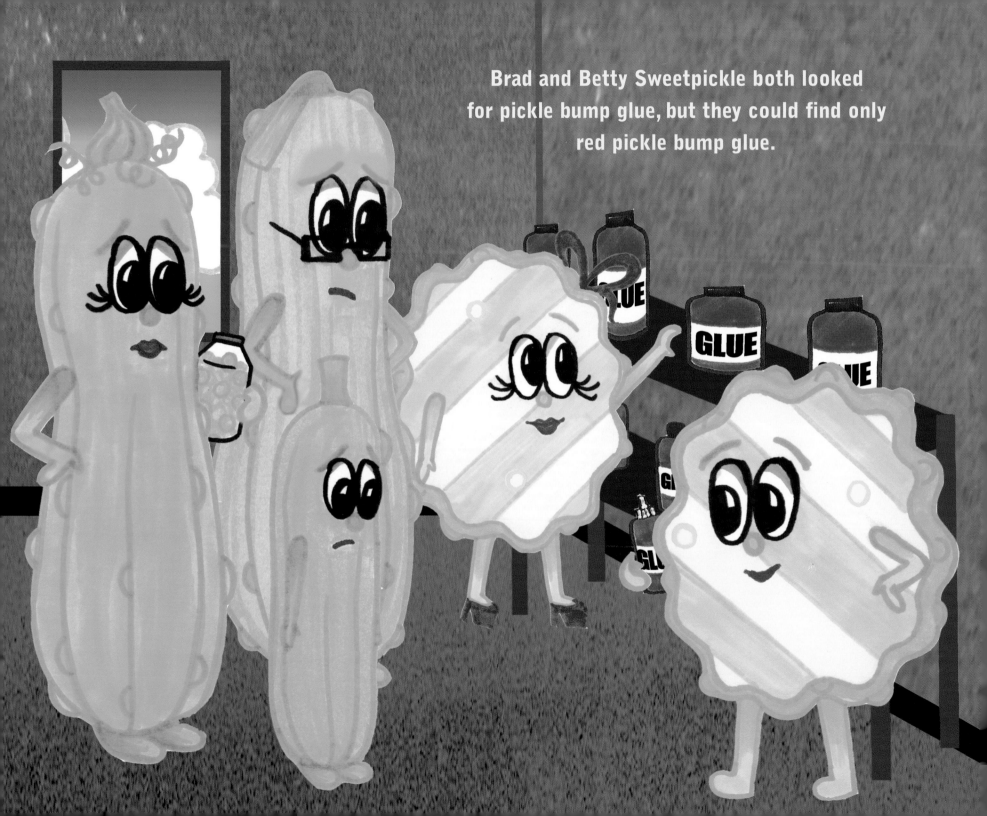

Brad and Betty Sweetpickle both looked for pickle bump glue, but they could find only red pickle bump glue.

Papa Dill said, "Red pickle bump glue won't work. We need green pickle bump glue. Baby Dill is green and the pickle bumps are green. We want the pickle bump glue to match."

Betty Sweetpickle told them that there was another pickle bump glue store across the street owned by Karl Kalamata. She thought that he might have green pickle bump glue.

So Mama and Papa Dill took Baby Dill across the street to see Karl Kalamata. They asked Karl Kalamata if he had any green pickle bump glue. Karl Kalamata said, "Oh, I am very sorry. I don't have any green pickle bump glue. However, I do have some blue pickle bump glue." "That won't work," said Mama Dill. "We need green pickle bump glue."

Karl Kalamata said, "Well, I also have yellow pickle bump glue."
So Karl Kalamata had blue pickle bump glue and yellow pickle bump glue,
but he did not have any green pickle bump glue.

Mama Dill said, "I have an idea. We could mix the blue pickle bump glue and the yellow pickle bump glue together."

"Because when you mix blue pickle bump glue and yellow pickle bump glue together, you get green pickle bump glue."

So, Mama and Papa Dill bought a jar of blue pickle bump glue and a jar of yellow pickle bump glue from Karl Kalamata and brought them home.

Mama and Papa Dill mixed the blue pickle bump glue with the yellow pickle bump glue and sure enough, they made green pickle bump glue.

Mama Dill called to Baby Dill,
"Baby Dill, come look!
We now have green pickle
bumps and green pickle bump
glue. Do you want us to glue
on your pickle bumps?"

Baby Dill was excited, and said, "Yes! But first I want to tell my friends!"

Baby Dill ran out of the house
to tell all the neighborhood
friends the good news.

Baby Dill told them that Mama and Papa Dill were
going to glue on some pickle bumps.

One of the friends said, "Baby Dill, don't do that! Then you will be just like all the other
dill pickle friends. You are different from them, and I think that is pretty neat."
Another friend said, "Yes! Look at all of us. We are all different too."
The other friends agreed, "We like you just the way you are!"

After playing for a while, Baby Dill went back into the house.
Mama Dill asked, "Do you want us to glue on your pickle bumps now?"
Baby Dill answered, "No. I'm going to stay just the way I am.
Not everybody can be the same, and I think it is okay to be different."
Papa Dill asked, "So, what are we going to do with the
pickle bumps and the pickle bump glue?"
Baby Dill said, "I have an idea!"

"We can glue them on the walls in my bedroom!"

Mama and Papa Dill thought that was a really good idea.
They all went into Baby Dill's bedroom to glue the pickle bumps onto the walls.

When they were done gluing all the pickle bumps on the walls, Baby Dill said, "Thank you Mama and Papa! My bedroom looks very nice. It's really different, just like me!"

Baby Dill was very happy!

About the Author

Bob Fulton is a Professor Emeritus at Saint John's University in Central Minnesota. He taught in the Saint John's University/College of Saint Benedict joint chemistry department for 39 years. His recent retirement allows him to spend more time traveling, visiting his children, and reading and telling stories to his grandchildren. He and his wife, Jackie, reside on Middle Spunk Lake in Avon, Minnesota.

About the Illustrator

Melissa Meyer is originally from Saint Joseph, Minnesota, but currently resides in La Crosse, Wisconsin with her fiancé, Stephen. She is a student at the University of Wisconsin-La Crosse. Melissa has dreamt of illustrating her first children's book for a long time and plans to continue work as a professional artist.

Baby Dill wonders what you have learned . . .

1. What was the name of the town where Baby Dill and his neighborhood friends lived?

2. What do the blocks that young Baby Dill was playing with spell?

3. What time was it when Baby Dill came in from the soccer field?

4. Who lived in the big stuffed-olive house?

5. Who owned The Pickle Bump Store?

6. Why didn't Mama and Papa Dill buy pickle bump glue from Brad and Betty Sweetpickle?

7. What did Mama and Papa Dill do when they could not find green pickle bump glue?

8. Why was Baby Dill so sad while the neighborhood friends were playing soccer?

9. What did Baby Dill's friends say about gluing on the pickle bumps?

10. What did Baby Dill finally decide to do with the pickle bumps?

11. Was there ever a time when you felt different from your friends?

12. What did you learn from this story?